CONTEXTING

RickyRussJr.com

The strangest thing happened last week. I found myself in heaven flipping through the Book of Life. This Book was nothing like I imagined over the years. And, it didn't contain just the names of people, but every last detail about them as well (By the way, God has the most amazing and perfect penmanship.)

The peculiar thing about each person's entry was at the end. It was almost like heaven's version of an email signature. Right below their names was their contact information. I was not expecting to see that.

Since I had randomly stopped in the P's while flipping through the Book, I thought I'd look to see if the Apostle Paul's name was there. It was. I found his name, and I immediately went to the end of his entry, and saw his phone number.

I quickly pulled out my phone and entered his number in my contacts. I wasn't sure if this was frowned upon in Heaven, so I looked around to see if anyone saw me do this.

At the same moment, I just so happen to see the Apostle Paul uploading his letters into the cloud. What are the odds?

I had so many questions about the letters he wrote. This moment was my chance to meet him. So, I casually flew over to him and introduced myself. He was very friendly and humble just like I imagined. I asked him,

"Do you have a moment for a few questions?"

He said with a smile,

"Ask away."

Then he said,

"By the way, I don't speak English, but since we are in heaven, we will understand each other anyway."

I thought I would have to spend some time thinking about his two statements, but then remembered there was no time in eternity and that I already knew what he meant. Weird.

Right before I asked my first question, I suddenly woke up. I realized it was all a dream, even though it seemed real. So real, that I grabbed my phone to see if Paul's number was in my contacts, and it was!

Then I thought I would text him and see what happens. You ready for this? He replied! We ended up texting for a long time (in earthly time). Below is our text thread conversation:

Hi Paul. My name is Ricky. Long story, but I found your phone number in my contacts.

Isn't it righteous that we are standing in line for the crown of righteousness, which the Lord, the righteous Judge, will award to me; and not only to me, but also to all who have loved His appearing?

Wait! That sounds familiar. Didn't you write those same words in 2 Timothy, chapter 4, verse 8?

2 Timothy? What do you mean Chapter 4? And verse 8?

Let's see. Where do I start? Many of the letters you wrote were put into The Holy Book along with Peter, John, Luke, James, Matthew, and Mark.

4

What about Barnabas' letter?
and Thomas' letter?

Yeah, they didn't make the cut.
Sorry.

Ok. Let's go back to the
chapter and verse part
because I only remember
writing two letters to Timothy.

About 1400 years after you
died, this one man came along
and decided to put numbers in
your letters to break up sections.
Then he added numbers to
your sentences which we
ended up calling verses.
Does that make sense?

No. Earlier when you said,
"2 Timothy, Chapter 4, Verse 8".
Are you telling me that
1400 years after I died, people
would refer to that one small

sentence by itself at the end of my letter opposed to what my letter was saying overall?

Unfortunately, yes.

Can you give me another example so I fully understand?

Ok. Here's a famous one. You remember in Romans when you said, ''And we know that God causes all things to work together for good to those who love God, to those who are called according to His purpose''?

Wow. That sentence shouldn't stand alone. If my memory serves me correctly, there were two sentences before that one which were part of my entire thought. Read those.

OK. Real quick - sorry, I forget you're in eternity and the word quick doesn't apply. Since we're already talking about Romans, can we discuss Chapter 7?

Haha. You're catching on. First, let's go back to referring to books as letters. That helps me. Second, you'll have to tell me what Chapter 7 references.

Deal. I'll call them letters. So, Chapter 7 has been a big topic of conversations for decades now. Especially verses 14 & 15.

That's funny.

This is the section where you said, "For we know that the Law is spiritual, but I am of flesh, sold into bondage to sin. For what I am doing, I do not understand; for I am not practicing what I would like to do, but I am doing the very thing I hate."

Let's end this whole chapter and verse thing. I'll make it very simple. Those who read the entire letter for themselves, it'll make sense to them. Those who read the "chapter and verse section", may die confused.

Fair enough. And actually, that makes a lot of sense.

Imagine if I had I started my letter to the Philippians with, "Not that I have already obtained it or have already become perfect, ...", nobody would've know what "it" was.

Great point. I just thought of another question. Why did you

write such a short letter
to Philemon?

First, I don't think your
memory serves you correctly
this time, because I didn't.

Oh yes you did. It's right
between Titus and Hebrews.

I don't know about this
Hebrews letter you
mentioned, but I think I
may know which letter
you're referring to.

I remember writing a letter
that opened with this, 'Paul,
a prisoner of Christ Jesus,
and Timothy our brother,
To Philemon our beloved
brother and fellow worker,
and to Apphia our sister,

and to Archippus our fellow soldier, and to the church in your house'. Is this the letter?

Yes. That's the letter you wrote to Philemon.

Did you read what I just typed? I said Philemon, Apphia, Archippus, and the church...

Oh! I see it now. Wait. Can you explain what you meant by "church in your house"? Because where I'm from, we "go to church".

Church was not a "place" that I was writing about. Church was basically a group of followers who met together in a house.

That makes sense. I guess after 2000 years, words and

meanings tend to change.

Did you say 2000 years?

Yes. I was born in 1976 AD.

That's amazing. I always thought Jesus was coming back in my time.

I think everyone for hundreds of years thought the same thing about their time.

I have another question for you. This question is about The Love Chapter.

Remember, I didn't write chapters. I wrote letters. Which letter are you referring to? I just want to be sure we are texting about the same thing.

Sorry. I keep forgetting. The chapter I'm referring to was in the 1st letter to the Corinthians.

Are you telling me if someone in your day simply says, "The Love Chapter", then everyone knows you're referring to one section in that one letter?

Yes. And not only that, but if you were to say, "verse 4", there are some people who would quote the following, "Love is patient, love is kind and is not jealous; love does not brag and is not arrogant,".

That's so interesting to me.

Yes. You're pretty famous

where I'm from. People quote you all the time.

That's not interesting to me. That actually makes me sad.

In the same letter as The Love Chapter you referred to, I said at the beginning,

"For I have been informed concerning you, my brethren, by Chloe's people, that there are quarrels among you. Now I mean this, that each one of you is saying, "I am of Paul," and "I of Apollos,"

and "I of Cephas," and "I of Christ." Has Christ been divided?" Was this part included in the letter you read?

I'm not sure. I don't think I read your entire letter. Most people just read individual chapters and memorize certain verses.

Are you saying that people memorize sentences in my letters?

Yes. Oh! You know how you were a custom tent designer?

No. What's a designer?

Umm. Let's see. Oh! You were a tent maker. Right?

Yes!

Anyway, people where I'm from put your famous sentences on their clothing.

14

I'm not sure how to respond to that. Give me an example.

Some people would have the following put on their shirt, "Phil 3:8"

What does that mean?

That's a famous verse from the book of Philippians.

You mean the letter to the Philippians?

Yes. I keep forgetting :)

What did I write in Phil 3:8?

You wrote, "More than that, I

count all things to be loss in view of the surpassing value of knowing Christ Jesus my Lord, for whom I have suffered the loss of all things, and count them but rubbish so that I may gain Christ,"

So, people would have all those words put on their shirt?

No. They just put the "Phil" followed by "3:8" on their shirt.

And everyone would know the words that Phil 3:8 refers to?

No. Most people would have to ask the person with the custom shirt to tell them what the verse was.

This really confuses me. Let's move to the next question.

16

Ok. In your second letter to the Thessalonians, you wrote, "nor did we eat anyone's bread without paying for it, but with labor and hardship we kept working night and day so that we would not be a burden to any of you;"

How did you work so much & still have time to preach?

That's an interesting question as well. When you "work night and day", you're normally around people and it's those people whom you proclaim good news. Does that make sense to you?

You're saying that all followers of Christ are doing ministry work when they share good news with while they work with them?

Exactly. I wrote about this in my letter to the Ephesians. Was that letter included in your collection of letters?

Yes! I think what you may be referring to is Eph. 4:11&12.

Again, tell me what I wrote in those verses.

Ok. "And He gave some as apostles, and some as prophets, and some as evangelists, and some as pastors and teachers, for the equipping of the saints for the work of service, to the building up of the body of Christ;"

Yes. That's a small piece of what I wrote to them. Is this what you call, "a famous verse"?

Very much so. Especially in the church. Well, I mean in the church building where the church gathers.

I was simply trying to tell the Ephesians that it's all about the equipping of the saints and how God has made EVERY follower either an apostle, prophet, evangelist, pastor, or teacher. It's that simple.

Wow. That makes complete sense now.

I have another question for you. Did you happen to read my first letter?

Yes. Of course. We all read Romans right after Acts.

Time out. What is Acts? And Romans wasn't my first letter.

I guess the easiest way to tell you about Acts is to tell you how it starts off. It says, "The first account I composed, Theophilus, about all that Jesus began to do and teach,".

Hmm. Which letter is before that in your collection of writings?

That would be Luke.

Well, maybe they should've named it 1st Luke because Acts should've been named 2nd Luke. Anyway, my first letter wasn't Romans. My first letter was to the Galatians.

Really?

Yes. Had you read my letters chronologically, they would've made more sense.

Hmm. I'm not sure why your letters were arranged in that order. Let's go back to what you called 2nd Luke. I have a question about Barnabas.

Ok. Did you happen to read his letter?

Uhh. What? Barnabas didn't write a letter.

He did. Even though he and I parted ways, I found his letter very encouraging. Was his letter not in your collection?

No. It was not included in the canon.

What is the canon?

Where do I start? Even though you are in eternity, that conversation would take forever.

Haha. But seriously. Are there famous writers in your day?

Yes. Have you met Billy Graham, Rick Warren, or DL Moody?

Yes. Did you read any of their letters?

Well, they wrote books, but yes I did.

Are any of their books in the canon?

No.

So, why did you read Billy, but not Barnabas?

That's a great question. I wonder if Gabriel has Barnabas' letter in his library?

I have another question for you.

Fire away.

Can you tell me who wrote Hebrews? I promise I won't tell anyone.

There was a reason this letter was left anonymous.

Ok. Fair enough. But there was a section in this letter that is also famous in my day, and I thought maybe you could interpret it for me.

Sure. I'll give it a try.

Ok. It says, "not forsaking our own assembling together, as is the habit of some, but encouraging one another; and all the more as you see the day drawing near."

Wait. You can't start a sentence with the word "Not".

What's the first word in the verse that precedes this one?

And

What about the verse that precedes that one?

Let

Ok. Now, before you ask me your question, do those three sentences together help you with the answer you're looking for?

Yes. That's cool.

I would encourage you to read what you call whole chapters. This sentence method is really not helping you.

Ok. I'm starting to catch a theme here :)

It's like I told Timothy, "You, however, continue in the things you have learned and become convinced of, knowing from whom you have learned them, and that from childhood you have

known the sacred writings which are able to give you the wisdom that leads to salvation through faith which is in Christ Jesus."

I'm surprised you didn't include the next sentence, "All Scripture is inspired by God and profitable for teaching, for reproof, for correction, for training in righteousness;"

The latter is formal where the former was personal for Timothy. Not every person has known the sacred writings from childhood.

Thanks for clarifying. That section makes more sense now as well.

Here's another one of your most famous verses, "I can do all things through Christ who strengthens me."

Is this on custom shirts as well?

Yes! People wear this when they exercise to remind themselves about how they can do all types of things relating to their sport.

Again, that sentence by itself falls short of what I was trying to say. I was referring to humble means, going hungry, and suffering need.

One doesn't need strengthening when he's already strengthened.

Can I quote you on that? I like that translation much better.

What do you mean by translation?

There are over 1000 options in 700 plus languages in your letters. People even argue between which ones are the most accurate. Pretty crazy, huh?

I don't even know how to process that.

Ok. Let's move on to another question then. In your second letter to the Corinthians, you wrote, "And even our gospel is veiled...", What did you mean by "our gospel"?

First, you know that "gospel" means good news, right?

I do now :)

Many people in my day had good news. Not all good news was The Good News. Would you agree?

Yes.

So, with that being said, and with you having read my letter, would you say I had good news of the glory of Christ to share?

Yes.

There's you answer. Everyone has their own "good news", and if their good news points to the good news about Christ,

then that's good news. So, they should share their gospel even if the god of this world blinds the minds of the unbelievers.

Now, that's gospel!

Would you like to hear a "Did You Know?"

I'd love to hear one.

Did you know that I didn't write Romans?

Stop the presses! What?

Nope. Sure didn't. Towards the end of the letter, it should read, "I, Tertius, who write this letter, greet you in the Lord."

Also, shortly after that it should read, "Now to Him who is able to establish you according to my gospel and the preaching of Jesus Christ, according to

the revelation of the mystery which has been kept secret for long ages past,".
I thought you may enjoy the "my gospel" part since you now know what I meant :)

So good! I'm glad we aren't running out of time since time doesn't exist. Back to Romans, I have another question.

I'll probably have the answer since I authored it.

Which sentence would you like to ask about?

"And do not be conformed to this world, but be transformed by the renewing of your mind, so that you may prove what the will of God is, that which is good and acceptable and perfect."

Before you ask your question, do you know the sentence that precedes the one you mentioned, since your's starts with "And"?

No. And I know what you're going to say, so I'll be sure to read it before I ask my question.

Here's a different question then. Did Jesus ever speak to you after Damascus? I don't remember you writing about it in any of your letters, if so.

Yes. One night in a vision He said, "Do not be afraid any longer, but go on speaking and do not be silent; for I am with you, and no man will attack you in order to harm you, for I have many people in this city."

Which letter was that?

It wasn't in my letters. These words were written in 2nd Luke.

Oh. I guess I should've read more than just your letters.

Hopefully you read the words of Jesus, right?

Yes. Of course. I read His words in the four gospels many times.

Four?

Yes. Matthew, Mark, Luke, and John.

So, you never read the gospel of Thomas?

I didn't know Thomas wrote a gospel. It's not in my collection of writings.

That's too bad. You really missed out. Thomas took a different approach than the other four guys. Thomas recorded a bunch of Jesus' sayings.

Can you share one with me?

Yes. Here's one of my favorites, "Jesus said, 'If the flesh came into being because of spirit, that is a marvel, but if spirit came into being because of the body, that is a marvel of marvels.'

Although that saying is really good and I can see how it runs parallel with the words of Jesus in The Gospels, I struggle, because it wasn't in the canon.

That's ok. Thomas wasn't the only one to doubt. It's not a salvation issue :)

Just remember to fight the good fight of faith; take hold of the eternal life to which you were called, and you made the good confession in the presence of many witnesses.

Yes. Thanks.

Do you have any more questions for me?

Yes. Many.

Ok. Keep asking.

There are many places in the Old Testament where it says not to drink wine or be drunk, but in your first letter to Timothy you wrote,

"No longer drink water exclusively, but use a little wine for the sake of your stomach and your frequent ailments."

Ok. So, two things. Who did I write the letter to?

Timothy.

Yes. What issue did he have?

He had frequent ailments.

Yes. Remember, this letter wasn't written to you. If it were written to you, I'd ask you if you "...remained on at Ephesus...," As well?

Well, that clears that up. So, what should be my takeaway from the entire letter you wrote to Timothy?

Here's how you will know: Write the whole letter out yourself. While doing so, remove all subheadings, chapter numbers, and verse numbers. After doing this, read it.

Then you'll see the takeaway.

Ok. That sounds like an exciting project.

I bet if you were to do this with some of my letters, while placing them in chronological order, they'd make more sense to you as well.

Ok. Do you happen to remember the chronological order off the top of your head?

Yes. Here they are:
Galatians. Thessalonians 1&2.
Corinthians 1&2.
Romans. Colossians. Philemon.
Ephesians. Philippians.
Timothy 1. Titus. Timothy 2.

Thanks.

Next question. Did you ever read the parable Jesus told about The Prodigal Son?

No. Over the years I heard many of Jesus' parables though. Of course, not all were recorded, but I'd love to hear the one you're referring to.

Ok. This parable was about the boy who left home only to return later to a happy dad and angry brother.

Oh! That parable. Yes. But, why did you call it, "The Prodigal Son"?

That was the subtitle written before verse 11 in Luke 15.

What? What's a subtitle? How are there words between your verse 10 and 11 when Jesus was telling back-to-back parables?

Great question. Something to think about for sure.

And if I remember correctly, the first sentence that Luke wrote was, "And He said, 'A man had two sons.'"

What's your point?

Maybe you should read Jesus' parable as "a man had two sons". It reads more accurately that way then the way your subtitle was written.

Oh. Gotcha! I'll do that.

It seems to me from all that you've shared so far, that my letters have lost their simplicity and have become much more confusing in your day.

It appears so. Do you have advice for me regarding that?

Yes. Like I once told Titus, "Avoid foolish controversies and genealogies and strife and disputes about the Law, for they are unprofitable and worthless." Think on this.

Anything else before my next question?

Yes. I always liked when John said the following in his first letter, "These things I have written to you concerning those who are trying to deceive you.

As for you, the anointing which you received from Him abides in you, and you have no need for anyone to teach you;

but as His anointing teaches you about all things, and is true and is not a lie, and just as it has taught you, you abide in Him."

What?! I've never heard that taught before.

Why would a teacher ever share a sentence with you about having no need for anyone to teach you?

Again, great point. Which leads me to my next question.

So, as we abide in Him, how do we know where to go?

It's just like I told the church in Corinth, "But thanks be to God, who always leads us in triumph in Christ, and manifests through us the sweet aroma of the

knowledge of Him in every place. For we are a fragrance of Christ to God among those who are being saved and among those who are perishing;"

It's no different than what Jesus said, "And as you go, preach, saying, 'The kingdom of heaven is at hand".

Exactly.

Except I don't remember you ever writing about "the Kingdom of God".

If you read the very last sentence in 2nd Luke, you will see that I stayed two full years in my own rented quarters and I was

welcoming all who came to me, preaching the kingdom of God and teaching concerning the Lord Jesus Christ with all openness, unhindered.

Once again, I stand corrected. It's amazing to me how listening to you is so different than listening to someone telling me about what they think you said.

Just like I told Timothy, the goal of our instruction is love from a pure heart and a good conscience and a sincere faith.

For some men, straying from these things, have turned aside to fruitless discussion, wanting to be teachers of the Law,

even though they do not understand either what they are saying or the matters about which they make confident assertions.

Do you believe that a true follower of Christ can be young and still accomplish this?

I say, let no one look down on your youthfulness, but rather in speech, conduct, love, faith and purity, show yourself an example of those who believe.

That's encouraging.

Also, remember to pay close attention to yourself and to your teaching;

persevere in these things, for as you do this you will ensure salvation both for yourself and for those who hear you.

Ok. Here's another question.

I thought you would have another question since we have yet to talk about the one thing that is probably still as much an issue in your day as it was in mine.

Which is?

Money.

Yup. This seems to rule everything around us here on earth.

Yes. Those who want to get rich fall into temptation and a snare and many foolish and harmful desires which plunge men into ruin and destruction.

That sounds familiar. Wait. Let me guess the next sentence. This is where you said something like, "For the love of money is the root of all sorts of evil".

No. To be accurate, I said, "For the love of money is a root of all sorts of evil,..."

Yeah. Same thing.

Actually, it isn't.

Explain.

You said "THE" root. I said "A" root. There are all sorts of evil.

The bad thing with money is that some by longing for it have wandered away from the faith and pierced themselves with many griefs.

I think I understand. Go on.

Obviously, there are some people who have money who haven't wandered away from the faith. Which means some have wandered away from the faith by other sorts of evil.

Wow! Yes. I think I spent too long believing money was evil because I remembered incorrectly what you said.

Just don't forget that godliness actually is a means of great gain when accompanied by contentment.

For we have brought nothing into the world, so we cannot take anything out of it either. If we have food and covering, with these we shall be content.

I hate to throw in a "yeah but...", but I'm going to, because I need clarification.

I understand.
Go ahead.

You said if anyone does not provide for his own, and especially for those of his household, he has denied the faith and is worse than an unbeliever.

I did, but the sentence which precedes the one you just mentioned should not be tied to this one.

If you have food and covering, more than likely it's because you're working; providing. If you have a household, and you're not working, then you're not providing.

That's why I told the Thessalonians,"...if anyone is not willing to work, then he is not to eat, either."

And there's the clarification

I needed. Thanks.

Hey. I can't seem to find anywhere in your letters where you mentioned tithing. Why is this?

I did. I just didn't use the word "tithing". For example, when I wrote to the Thess-alonians, I talked about excelling in love.

I'm not following.

I told them when they excel in love they will behave properly toward outsiders and not be in any need.

Oh! That sounds much like some of Malachi's writings.

Yes. Outsiders can be widows, orphans, and those who are oppressed. God blesses the work of our hands so we can bless them.

Gotcha. I now see how what you wrote ties in with what Malachi was writing about.

That's why you have no need for anyone to write to you, for you yourselves are taught by God to love one another.

By the way, I'm highlighting these sections in my Holy Book to refer to later.

That's good to hear.

Did you ever deal with confirmation bias during your time on earth?

Define that for me.

Confirmation bias is the tendency to search for, interpret, favor, and recall information in a way that confirms one's preexisting beliefs.

Of course. Even Jesus did.

Can you give me an example where Jesus dealt with this?

Yes. I believe Matthew wrote, "And they took offense at Him. But Jesus said to them,

"A prophet is not without honor except in his home-town and in his own house-hold." And He did not do many miracles there because of their unbelief."

That's amazing. Which chapter in Matthew were these words written?

You'll have to search Matthew's gospel to find them. Be like the Bereans.

Fair enough. I had a feeling you would say that.

Next question. Did you ever teach your followers to fast?

No.

Why not? Jesus did.

You may want to re-read the gospels according to His disciples before believing that.

I definitely will because many today teach that He did.

Would you like another Did You Know?

I love these. Yes!

Did you know Jesus didn't pray with His disciples?

Now, this one is tough to believe. Not saying I can't, but it will be hard. Explain.

I once remember my buddy Luke showing me a section of his writings. It read,

"It happened that while Jesus was praying in a certain place, after He had finished, one of His disciples said to

Him, "Lord, teach us to pray just as John also taught his disciples."

Break this down for me.

If you do something with someone month after month, there's no need to teach them. Would you agree?

Yes. That makes sense.

Countless times Jesus would go away alone to pray.

Some may argue that it doesn't mean He didn't pray with them though.

Of course some will argue, but assuming something that's not written is dangerous too.

True. Either way, I could read your Did You Know questions all day.

How many people did you lead to Jesus during all your travels?

You ask some strange questions. But, to answer your question, I guess I'd say zero.

Is that an auto correct? Did you really mean to type the word zero?

Maybe you'll remember this, "I planted, Apollos watered, but God was causing the growth. So then neither the one who plants nor the one who waters is anything, but God who causes the growth."

Yes. I do remember reading that.

You are God's fellow workers; you are God's field, God's building.

That's a great reminder!

Here's a random question. Did you guys ever tell jokes?

Not sure. Tell me one.

Ok. How about this one. What did Jesus say to Malchus after re-attaching the ear that Peter cut off with a sword? "He who has ears, let him hear."

How do you know this?

Nevermind. Let's move on.

We've been texting for a while now. How's your battery life?

I'm not sure what you mean.

In the top right corner of your phone, there should be a number. It represents how much battery life remains.

Oh! Don't forget, anything based on time doesn't exist in heaven. This is the only thing in the top right section on my phone: ∞

Of course :)

Before we move to your next question, I have a few for you.

Really? Cool! I'd love to hear what type of questions you have for me.

You said earlier that you are from a time around 2000 AD?

Yes. And to be accurate, the current year is 2017.

Ok. Since you know my gospel, I'd love to hear your gospel!

Do you mind if I share a short story with you? It's one of the ways I share my gospel.

Sure. I like stories.

Years ago, I was making horrible decisions. I walked

around with a lack of knowledge. Then one day I met a Life Coach. In order to learn from Him, I had to walk away from myself. When I did, He taught me about life. He gave me knowledge and showed me love.

Later, my past caught up with me. I was arrested for my past crimes. Then I was given life in prison.

I cried out for forgiveness from my cell. Miraculously I was freed four days later. Upon being released, I ran to His house.

I wanted to tell Him that I was free, but, He was nowhere to be found. Then I found a letter on His table.

His letter explained what He did for me. I couldn't believe He would do that for me.

It was such a bitter sweet revelation, because I was free even though He was gone.

Somehow there was comfort in my spirit. Then, I remembered what He told me.

So, I continued to follow His coaching. I began to tell others all that He coached me. Today, I'm a Life Coach too.

That is good news! Are you currently writing letters to anyone?

Yes. I have a close friend who is in prison right now.

Have you been to prison?

Well, not in the way you know the word prison. In 2017, more people live in a mental prison then they do in an actual prison like you did.

Is there a way for you to show me what my writings look like in 2017?

I can send you a couple of screen shots if you'd like.

Screen shots?

Hmm. I'm not sure how to explain screen shots. I'll just send you an image after this sentence. Here is a sample of what we read:

God's Marvelous Plan for the Gentiles

3 For this reason I, Paul, the prisoner of Christ Jesus for the sake of you Gentiles—

2 Surely you have heard about the administration of God's grace that was given to me for you, 3 that is, the mystery made known to me by revelation, as I have already written briefly. 4 In reading this, then, you will be able to understand my insight into the mystery of Christ, 5 which was not made known to people in other generations as it has now been revealed by the Spirit to God's holy apostles and prophets. 6 This mystery is that through the gospel the Gentiles are heirs together with Israel, members together of one body, and sharers together in the promise in Christ Jesus.

7 I became a servant of this gospel by the gift of God's grace given me through the working of his power. 8 Although I am less than the least of all the Lord's people, this grace was given me: to preach to the Gentiles the boundless riches of Christ, 9 and to make plain to everyone the administration of this mystery, which for ages past was kept hidden in God, who created all things. 10 His intent was that now, through the church, the manifold wisdom of God should be made known to the rulers and authorities in the heavenly realms, 11 according to his eternal purpose that he accomplished in Christ Jesus our Lord. 12 In him and through faith in him we may approach God with freedom and confidence. 13 I ask you, therefore, not to be discouraged because of my sufferings for you, which are your glory.

After seeing that, I think you should still strongly consider the project we discussed earlier.

If you move forward, start with three cities and three men.

Which letters do you recommend for this project?

Start with these in this order: Galatians, Thessalonians 1, Corinthians 1, Philemon, Timothy 1, and Titus.

OK. Also, can I share our conversation with others?

Yes. It may cause some people to read my letters again from a different perspective.

Sweet. So, here's my idea. I'll place our entire conversation in a book, and then I'll put the project you tasked me with at the end.

I like that idea. Go for it.

Well, I better get to work then. Thanks for contexting w/ me.

When you finish, text me, and we can do more Q&A. I'm sure you'll have questions after reading my letters without all the numbers and subtitles. #contexting

Paul, an apostle sent not from men nor by a man, but by Jesus Christ and God the Father, who raised him from the dead and all the brothers and sisters with me, To the churches in Galatia. Grace and peace to you from God our Father and the Lord Jesus Christ, who gave himself for our sins to rescue us from the present evil age, according to the will of our God and Father, to whom be glory for ever and ever. Amen. I am astonished that you are so quickly deserting the one who called you to live in the grace of Christ and are turning to a different gospel which is really no gospel at all. Evidently some people are throwing you into confusion and are trying to pervert the gospel of Christ. But even if we or an angel from heaven should preach a gospel other than the one we preached to you, let them be under God's curse.

As we have already said, so now I say again: If anybody is preaching to you a gospel other than what you accepted, let them be under God's curse. Am I now trying to win the approval of human beings, or of God? Or am I trying to please people? If I were still trying to please people, I would not be a servant of Christ. I want you to know, brothers and sisters, that the gospel I preached is not of human origin. I did not receive it from any man, nor was I taught it; rather, I received it by revelation from Jesus Christ. For you have heard of my previous way of life in Judaism, how intensely I persecuted the church of God and tried to destroy it. I was advancing in Judaism beyond many of my own age among my people and was extremely zealous for the traditions of my fathers. But when God, who set me apart from my mother's womb and called me by his grace, was pleased to reveal his Son in me so that I might preach him among the Gentiles, my immediate response was not to consult any human being. I did not go up to Jerusalem to see those who were apostles before I was, but I went into Arabia. Later I returned to Damascus. Then after three years, I went up to Jerusalem to get acquainted with Cephas and stayed with him fifteen days. I saw none of the other apostles only James, the Lord's brother. I assure you before God that what I am writing you is no lie. Then I went to Syria and Cilicia. I was personally unknown to the churches of Judea that are in Christ. They only heard the report: "The man who formerly persecuted us is now preaching the faith he once tried to destroy." And they praised God because of me.

Then after fourteen years, I went up again to Jerusalem, this time with Barnabas. I took Titus along also. I went in response to a revelation and, meeting privately with those esteemed as leaders, I presented to them the gospel that I preach among the Gentiles. I wanted to be sure I was not running and had not been running my race in vain. Yet not even Titus, who was with me, was compelled to be circumcised, even though he was a Greek. This matter arose because some false believers had infiltrated our ranks to spy on the freedom we have in Christ Jesus and to make us slaves. We did not give in to them for a moment, so that the truth of the gospel might be preserved for you. As for those who were held in high esteem—whatever they were makes no difference to me; God does not show favoritism—they added nothing to my message. On the contrary, they recognized that I had been entrusted with the task of preaching the gospel to the uncircumcised, just as Peter had been to the circumcised. For God, who was at work in Peter as an apostle to the circumcised, was also at work in me as an apostle to the Gentiles. James, Cephas and John, those esteemed as pillars, gave me and Barnabas the right hand of fellowship when they recognized the grace given to me. They agreed that we should go to the Gentiles, and they to the circumcised. All they asked was that we should continue to remember the poor, the very thing I had been eager to do all along. When Cephas came to Antioch, I opposed him to his face, because he stood condemned. For before certain men came from James, he used to eat with the Gentiles. But when they arrived, he began to draw back and separate himself from the Gentiles because he was afraid of those who belonged to the circumcision group. The other Jews joined him in his hypocrisy, so that by their hypocrisy even Barnabas was led astray. When I saw that they were not acting in line with the truth of the gospel, I said to Cephas in front of them all, "You are a Jew, yet you live like a Gentile and not like a Jew. How is it, then, that you force Gentiles to follow Jewish customs? We who are Jews by birth and not sinful Gentiles know that a person is not justified by the works of the law, but by faith in Jesus Christ.

So we, too, have put our faith in Christ Jesus that we may be justified by faith in Christ and not by the works of the law, because by the works of the law no one will be justified. But if, in seeking to be justified in Christ, we Jews find ourselves also among the sinners, doesn't that mean that Christ promotes sin? Absolutely not! If I rebuild what I destroyed, then I really would be a lawbreaker. For through the law I died to the law so that I might live for God. I have been crucified with Christ and I no longer live, but Christ lives in me. The life I now live in the body, I live by faith in the Son of God, who loved me and gave himself for me. I do not set aside the grace of God, for if righteousness could be gained through the law, Christ died for nothing!

You foolish Galatians! Who has bewitched you? Before your very eyes Jesus Christ was clearly portrayed as crucified. I would like to learn just one thing from you: Did you receive the Spirit by the works of the law, or by believing what you heard? Are you so foolish? After beginning by means of the Spirit, are you now trying to finish by means of the flesh? Have you experienced so much in vain if it really was in vain? So again I ask, does God give you his Spirit and work miracles among you by the works of the law, or by your believing what you heard? So also Abraham "believed God, and it was credited to him as righteousness. Understand, then, that those who have faith are children of Abraham.

Scripture foresaw that God would justify the Gentiles by faith, and announced the gospel in advance to Abraham: "All nations will be blessed through you."So those who rely on faith are blessed along with Abraham, the man of faith. For all who rely on the works of the law are under a curse, as it is written: "Cursed is everyone who does not continue to do everything written in the Book of the Law."Clearly no one who relies on the law is justified before God, because "the righteous will live by faith."The law is not based on faith; on the contrary, it says, "The person who does these things will live by them."Christ redeemed us from the curse of the law by becoming a curse for us, for it is written: "Cursed is everyone who is hung on a pole." He redeemed us in order that the blessing given to Abraham might come to the Gentiles through Christ Jesus, so that by faith we might receive the promise of the Spirit. Brothers and sisters, let me take an example from everyday life. Just as no one can set aside or add to a human covenant that has been duly established, so it is in this case. The promises were spoken to Abraham and to his seed.

Scripture does not say "and to seeds," meaning many people, but "and to your seed," meaning one person, who is Christ. What I mean is this: The law, introduced 430 years later, does not set aside the covenant previously established by God and thus do away with the promise. For if the inheritance depends on the law, then it no longer depends on the promise; but God in his grace gave it to Abraham through a promise. Why, then, was the law given at all? It was added because of transgressions until the Seed to whom the promise referred had come. The law was given through angels and entrusted to a mediator. A mediator, however, implies more than one party; but God is one. Is the law, therefore, opposed to the promises of God? Absolutely not! For if a law had been given that could impart life, then righteousness would certainly have come by the law. But Scripture has locked up everything under the control of sin, so that what was promised, being given through faith in Jesus Christ, might be given to those who believe. Before the coming of this faith, we were held in custody under the law, locked up until the faith that was to come would be revealed. So the law was our guardian until Christ came that we might be justified by faith. Now that this faith has come, we are no longer under a guardian. So in Christ Jesus you are all children of God through faith, for all of you who were baptized into Christ have clothed yourselves with Christ. There is neither Jew nor Gentile, neither slave nor free, nor is there male and female, for you are all one in Christ Jesus. If you belong to Christ, then you are Abraham's seed, and heirs according to the promise.

What I am saying is that as long as an heir is underage, he is no different from a slave, although he owns the whole estate. The heir is subject to guardians and trustees until the time set by his father. So also, when we were underage, we were in slavery under the elemental spiritual forces of the world. But when the set time had fully come, God sent his Son, born of a woman, born under the law, to redeem those under the law, that we might receive adoption to sonship. Because you are his sons, God sent the Spirit of his Son into our hearts, the Spirit who calls out, "Abba, Father." So you are no longer a slave, but God's child; and since you are his child, God has made you also an heir. Formerly, when you did not know God, you were slaves to those who by nature are not gods. But now that you know God—or rather are known by God—how is it that you are turning back to those weak and miserable forces? Do you wish to be enslaved by them all over again? You are observing special days and months and seasons and years! I fear for you, that somehow I have wasted my efforts on you. I plead with you, brothers and sisters, become like me, for I became like you. You did me no wrong. As you know, it was because of an illness that I first preached the gospel to you, and even though my illness was a trial to you, you did not treat me with contempt or scorn. Instead, you welcomed me as if I were an angel of God, as if I were Christ Jesus himself. Where, then, is your blessing of me now? I can testify that, if you could have done so, you would have torn out your eyes and given them to me. Have I now become your enemy by telling you the truth? Those people are zealous to win you over, but for no good. What they want is to alienate you from us, so that you may have zeal for them. It is fine to be zealous, provided the purpose is good, and to be so always, not just when I am with you.

My dear children, for whom I am again in the pains of childbirth until Christ is formed in you, how I wish I could be with you now and change my tone, because I am perplexed about you! Tell me, you who want to be under the law, are you not aware of what the law says? For it is written that Abraham had two sons, one by the slave woman and the other by the free woman. His son by the slave woman was born according to the flesh, but his son by the free woman was born as the result of a divine promise. These things are being taken figuratively: The women represent two covenants. One covenant is from Mount Sinai and bears children who are to be slaves: This is Hagar. Now Hagar stands for Mount Sinai in Arabia and corresponds to the present city of Jerusalem, because she is in slavery with her children. But the Jerusalem that is above is free, and she is our mother. For it is written: "Be glad, barren woman, you who never bore a child; shout for joy and cry aloud, you who were never in labor; because more are the children of the desolate woman than of her who has a husband." Now you, brothers and sisters, like Isaac, are children of promise. At that time the son born according to the flesh persecuted the son born by the power of the Spirit. It is the same now. But what does Scripture say? "Get rid of the slave woman and her son, for the slave woman's son will never share in the inheritance with the free woman's son." Therefore, brothers and sisters, we are not children of the slave woman, but of the free woman.

It is for freedom that Christ has set us free. Stand firm, then, and do not let yourselves be burdened again by a yoke of slavery. Mark my words! I, Paul, tell you that if you let yourselves be circumcised, Christ will be of no value to you at all. Again I declare to every man who lets himself be circumcised that he is obligated to obey the whole law. You who are trying to be justified by the law have been alienated from Christ; you have fallen away from grace. For through the Spirit we eagerly await by faith the righteousness for which we hope. For in Christ Jesus neither circumcision nor uncircumcision has any value. The only thing that counts is faith expressing itself through love. You were running a good race. Who cut in on you to keep you from obeying the truth? That kind of persuasion does not come from the one who calls you. "A little yeast works through the whole batch of dough." I am confident in the Lord that you will take no other view.

The one who is throwing you into confusion, whoever that may be, will have to pay the penalty. Brothers and sisters, if I am still preaching circumcision, why am I still being persecuted? In that case the offense of the cross has been abolished. As for those agitators, I wish they would go the whole way and emasculate themselves! You, my brothers and sisters, were called to be free. But do not use your freedom to indulge the flesh; rather, serve one another humbly in love. For the entire law is fulfilled in keeping this one command: "Love your neighbor as yourself." If you bite and devour each other, watch out or you will be destroyed by each other.

So I say, walk by the Spirit, and you will not gratify the desires of the flesh. For the flesh desires what is contrary to the Spirit, and the Spirit what is contrary to the flesh. They are in conflict with each other, so that you are not to do whatever you want. But if you are led by the Spirit, you are not under the law. The acts of the flesh are obvious: sexual immorality, impurity and debauchery; idolatry and witchcraft; hatred, discord, jealousy, fits of rage, selfish ambition, dissensions, factions and envy; drunkenness, orgies, and the like. I warn you, as I did before, that those who live like this will not inherit the kingdom of God. But the fruit of the Spirit is love, joy, peace, forbearance, kindness, goodness, faithfulness, gentleness and self-control. Against such things there is no law. Those who belong to Christ Jesus have crucified the flesh with its passions and desires. Since we live by the Spirit, let us keep in step with the Spirit. Let us not become conceited, provoking and envying each other.

Brothers and sisters, if someone is caught in a sin, you who live by the Spirit should restore that person gently. But watch yourselves, or you also may be tempted. Carry each other's burdens, and in this way you will fulfill the law of

Christ. If anyone thinks they are something when they are not, they deceive themselves. Each one should test their own actions. Then they can take pride in themselves alone, without comparing themselves to someone else, for each one should carry their own load. Nevertheless, the one who receives instruction in the word should share all good things with their instructor.

Do not be deceived: God cannot be mocked. A man reaps what he sows. Whoever sows to please their flesh, from the flesh will reap destruction; whoever sows to please the Spirit, from the Spirit will reap eternal life. Let us not become weary in doing good, for at the proper time we will reap a harvest if we do not give up. Therefore, as we have opportunity, let us do good to all people, especially to those who belong to the family of believers. See what large letters I use as I write to you with my own hand! Those who want to impress people by means of the flesh are trying to compel you to be circumcised. The only reason they do this is to avoid being persecuted for the cross of Christ. Not even those who are circumcised keep the law, yet they want you to be circumcised that they may boast about your circumcision in the flesh. May I never boast except in the cross of our Lord Jesus Christ, through which the world has been crucified to me, and I to the world. Neither circumcision nor uncircumcision means anything; what counts is the new creation. Peace and mercy to all who follow this rule—to the Israel of God. From now on, let no one cause me trouble, for I bear on my body the marks of Jesus. The grace of our Lord Jesus Christ be with your spirit, brothers and sisters. Amen.

Paul, Silas and Timothy, To the church of the Thessalonians in God the Father and the Lord Jesus Christ: Grace and peace to you. We always thank God for all of you and continually mention you in our prayers. We remember before our God and Father your work produced by faith, your labor prompted by love, and your endurance inspired by hope in our Lord Jesus Christ. For we know, brothers and sisters loved by God, that he has chosen you, because our gospel came to you not simply with words but also with power, with the Holy Spirit and deep conviction. You know how we lived among you for your sake. You became imitators of us and of the Lord, for you welcomed the message in the midst of severe suffering with the joy given by the Holy Spirit. And so you became a model to all the believers in Macedonia and Achaia. The Lord's message rang out from you not only in Macedonia and Achaia—your faith in God has become known everywhere. Therefore we do not need to say anything about it, for they themselves report what kind of reception you gave us. They tell how you turned to God from idols to serve the living and true God, and to wait for his Son from heaven, whom he raised from the dead—Jesus, who rescues us from the coming wrath.

You know, brothers and sisters, that our visit to you was not without results. We had previously suffered and been treated outrageously in Philippi, as you know, but with the help of our God we dared to tell you his gospel in the face of strong opposition. For the appeal we make does not spring from error or impure motives, nor are we trying to trick you. On the contrary, we speak as those approved by God to be entrusted with the gospel. We are not trying to please people but God, who tests our hearts. You know we never used flattery, nor did we put on a mask to cover up greed—God is our witness. We were not looking for praise from people, not from you or anyone else, even though as apostles of Christ we could have asserted our authority. Instead, we were like young children among you. Just as a nursing mother cares for her children, so we cared for you. Because we loved you so much, we were delighted to share with you not only the gospel of God but our lives as well.

Surely you remember, brothers and sisters, our toil and hardship; we worked night and day in order not to be a burden to anyone while we preached the gospel of God to you. You are witnesses, and so is God, of how holy, righteous and blameless we were among you who believed. For you know that we dealt with each of you as a father deals with his own children, encouraging, comforting and urging you to live lives worthy of God, who calls you into his kingdom and glory. And we also thank God continually because, when you received the word of God, which you heard from us, you accepted it not as a human word, but as it actually is, the word of God, which is indeed at work in you who believe. For you, brothers and sisters, became imitators of God's churches in Judea, which are in Christ Jesus: You suffered from your own people the same things those churches suffered from the Jews who killed the Lord Jesus and the prophets and also drove us out. They displease God and are hostile to everyone in their effort to keep us from speaking to the Gentiles so that they may be saved. In this way they always heap up their sins to the limit. The wrath of God has come upon them at last. But, brothers and sisters, when we were orphaned by being separated from you for a short time (in person, not in thought), out of our intense longing we made every effort to see you. For we wanted to come to you—certainly I, Paul, did, again and again—but Satan blocked our way. For what is our hope, our joy, or the crown in which we will glory in the presence of our Lord Jesus when he comes? Is it not you? Indeed, you are our glory and joy.

So when we could stand it no longer, we thought it best to be left by ourselves in Athens. We sent Timothy, who is our brother and co-worker in God's service in spreading the gospel of Christ, to strengthen and encourage you in your faith, so that no one would be unsettled by these trials. For you know quite well that we are destined for them. In fact, when we were with you, we kept telling you that we would be persecuted. And it turned out that way, as you well know. For this reason, when I could stand it no longer, I sent to find out about your faith. I was afraid that in some way the tempter had tempted you and that our labors might have been in vain. But Timothy has just now come to us from you and has brought good news about your faith and love. He has told us that you always have pleasant memories of us and that you long to see us, just as we also long to see you.

Therefore, brothers and sisters, in all our distress and persecution we were encouraged about you because of your faith. For now we really live, since you are standing firm in the Lord. How can we thank God enough for you in return for all the joy we have in the presence of our God because of you? Night and day we pray most earnestly that we may see you again and supply what is lacking in your faith. Now may our God and Father himself and our Lord Jesus clear the way for us to come to you. May the Lord make your love increase and overflow for each other and for everyone else, just as ours does for you. May he strengthen your hearts so that you will be blameless and holy in the presence of our God and Father when our Lord Jesus comes with all his holy ones.

As for other matters, brothers and sisters, we instructed you how to live in order to please God, as in fact you are living. Now we ask you and urge you in the Lord Jesus to do this more and more. For you know what instructions we gave you by the authority of the Lord Jesus. It is God's will that you should be sanctified: that you should avoid sexual immorality; that each of you should learn to control your own body in a way that is holy and honorable, not in passionate lust like the pagans, who do not know God; and that in this matter no one should wrong or take advantage of a brother or sister. The Lord will punish all those who commit such sins, as we told you and warned you before. For God did not call us to be impure, but to live a holy life. Therefore, anyone who rejects this instruction does not reject a human being but God, the very God who gives you his Holy Spirit. Now about your love for one another we do not need to write to you, for you yourselves have been taught by God to love each other. And in fact, you do love all of God's family throughout Macedonia. Yet we urge you, brothers and sisters, to do so more and more, and to make it your ambition to lead a quiet life: You should mind your own business and work with your hands, just as we told you, so that your daily life may win the respect of outsiders and so that you will not be dependent on anybody. Brothers and sisters, we do not want you to be uninformed about those who sleep in death, so that you do not grieve like the rest of mankind, who have no hope. For we believe that Jesus died and rose again, and so we believe that God will bring with Jesus those who have fallen asleep in him. According to the Lord's word, we tell you that we who are still alive, who are left until the coming of the Lord, will certainly not precede those who have fallen asleep. For the Lord himself will come down from heaven, with a loud command, with the voice of the archangel and with the trumpet call of God, and the dead in Christ will rise first. After that, we who are still alive and are left will be caught up together with them in the clouds to meet the Lord in the air. And so we will be with the Lord forever. Therefore encourage one another with these words.

Now, brothers and sisters, about times and dates we do not need to write to you, or you know very well that the day of the Lord will come like a thief in the night. While people are saying, "Peace and safety," destruction will come on them suddenly, as labor pains on a pregnant woman, and they will not escape. But you, brothers and sisters, are not in darkness so that this day should surprise you like a thief. You are all children of the light and children of the day. We do not belong to the night or to the darkness. So then, let us not be like others, who are asleep, but let us be awake and sober. For those who sleep, sleep at night, and those who get drunk, get drunk at night. But since we belong to the day, let us be sober, putting on faith and love as a breastplate, and the hope of salvation as a helmet. For God did not appoint us to suffer wrath but to receive salvation through our Lord Jesus Christ. He died for us so that, whether we are awake or asleep, we may live together with him. Therefore encourage one another and build each other up, just as in fact you are doing.

Now we ask you, brothers and sisters, to acknowledge those who work hard among you, who care for you in the Lord and who admonish you. Hold them in the highest regard in love because of their work. Live in peace with each other. And we urge you, brothers and sisters, warn those who are idle and disruptive, encourage the disheartened, help the weak, be patient with everyone. Make sure that nobody pays back wrong for wrong, but always strive to do what is good for each other and for everyone else. Rejoice always, pray continually, give thanks in all circumstances; for this is God's will for you in Christ Jesus. Do not quench the Spirit. Do not treat prophecies with contempt but test them all; hold on to what is good, reject every kind of evil. May God himself, the God of peace, sanctify you through and through. May your whole spirit, soul and body be kept blameless at the coming of our Lord Jesus Christ. The one who calls you is faithful, and he will do it. Brothers and sisters, pray for us. Greet all God's people with a holy kiss. I charge you before the Lord to have this letter read to all the brothers and sisters. The grace of our Lord Jesus Christ be with you.

Paul, called to be an apostle of Christ Jesus by the will of God, and our brother Sosthenes, to the church of God in Corinth, to those sanctified in Christ Jesus and called to be his holy people, together with all those everywhere who call on the name of our Lord Jesus Christ—their Lord and ours: Grace and peace to you from God our Father and the Lord Jesus Christ. I always thank my God for you because of his grace given you in Christ Jesus. For in him you have been enriched in every way—with all kinds of speech and with all knowledge— God thus confirming our testimony about Christ among you. Therefore you do not lack any spiritual gift as you eagerly wait for our Lord Jesus Christ to be revealed. He will also keep you firm to the end, so that you will be blameless on the day of our Lord Jesus Christ. God is faithful, who has called you into fellowship with his Son, Jesus Christ our Lord.

I appeal to you, brothers and sisters, in the name of our Lord Jesus Christ, that all of you agree with one another in what you say and that there be no divisions among you, but that you be perfectly united in mind and thought. My brothers and sisters, some from Chloe's household have informed me that there are quarrels among you. What I mean is this: One of you says, "I follow Paul"; another, "I follow Apollos"; another, "I follow Cephas"; still another, "I follow Christ." Is Christ divided? Was Paul crucified for you? Were you baptized in the name of Paul? I thank God that I did not baptize any of you except Crispus and Gaius, so no one can say that you were baptized in my name. (Yes,

I also baptized the household of Stephanas; beyond that, I don't remember if I baptized anyone else.) For Christ did not send me to baptize, but to preach the gospel—not with wisdom and eloquence, lest the cross of Christ be emptied of its power.

For the message of the cross is foolishness to those who are perishing, but to us who are being saved it is the power of God. For it is written: "I will destroy the wisdom of the wise; the intelligence of the intelligent I will frustrate."Where is the wise person? Where is the teacher of the law? Where is the philosopher of this age? Has not God made foolish the wisdom of the world? For since in the wisdom of God the world through its wisdom did not know him, God was pleased through the foolishness of what was preached to save those who believe. Jews demand signs and Greeks look for wisdom, but we preach Christ crucified: a stumbling block to Jews and foolishness to Gentiles, but to those whom God has called, both Jews and Greeks, Christ the power of God and the wisdom of God. For the foolishness of God is wiser than human wisdom, and the weakness of God is stronger than human strength.

Brothers and sisters, think of what you were when you were called. Not many of you were wise by human standards; not many were influential; not many were of noble birth. But God chose the foolish things of the world to shame the wise; God chose the weak things of the world to shame the strong. God chose the lowly things of this world and the despised things—and the things that are not—to nullify the things that are, so that no one may boast before him.

It is because of him that you are in Christ Jesus, who has become for us wisdom from God—that is, our righteousness, holiness and redemption. Therefore, as it is written: "Let the one who boasts boast in the Lord."

And so it was with me, brothers and sisters. When I came to you, I did not come with eloquence or human wisdom as I proclaimed to you the testimony about God. For I resolved to know nothing while I was with you except Jesus Christ and him crucified. I came to you in weakness with great fear and trembling. My message and my preaching were not with wise and persuasive words, but with a demonstration of the Spirit's power, so that your faith might not rest on human wisdom, but on God's power. We do, however, speak a message of wisdom among the mature, but not the wisdom of this age or of the rulers of this age, who are coming to nothing. No, we declare God's wisdom, a mystery that has been hidden and that God destined for our glory before time began. None of the rulers of this age understood it, for if they had, they would not have crucified the Lord of glory.

However, as it is written: "What no eye has seen, what no ear has heard, and what no human mind has conceived" — the things God has prepared for those who love him — these are the things God has revealed to us by his Spirit. The Spirit searches all things, even the deep things of God. For who knows a person's thoughts except their own spirit within them? In the same way no one knows the thoughts of God except the Spirit of God. What we have received is not the spirit of the world, but the Spirit who is from God, so that we may understand what God has freely given us. This is what we speak, not in words taught us by human wisdom but in words taught by the Spirit, explaining spiritual realities with Spirit-taught words. The person without the Spirit does not accept the things that come from the Spirit of God but considers them foolishness, and cannot understand them because they are discerned only through the Spirit. The person with the Spirit makes judgments about all things, but such a person is not subject to merely human judgments, for, "Who has known the mind of the Lord so as to instruct him?" But we have the mind of Christ.

Brothers and sisters, I could not address you as people who live by the Spirit but as people who are still worldly—mere infants in Christ. I gave you milk, not solid food, for you were not yet ready for it. Indeed, you are still not ready. You are still worldly. For since there is jealousy and quarreling among you, are you not worldly? Are you not acting like mere humans? For when one says, "I follow Paul," and another, "I follow Apollos," are you not mere human beings? What, after all, is Apollos? And what is Paul? Only servants, through whom you came to believe—as the Lord has assigned to each his task. I planted the seed, Apollos watered it, but God has been making it grow. So neither the one who plants nor the one who waters is anything, but only God, who makes things grow. The one who plants and the one who waters have one purpose, and they will each be rewarded according to their own labor. For we are co-workers in God's service; you are God's field, God's building. By the grace God has given me, I laid a foundation as a wise builder, and someone else is building on it.

But each one should build with care. For no one can lay any foundation other than the one already laid, which is Jesus Christ. If anyone builds on this foundation using gold, silver, costly stones, wood, hay or straw, their work will be shown for what it is, because the Day will bring it to light. It will be revealed with fire, and the fire will test the quality of each person's work. If what has been built survives, the builder will receive a reward. If it is burned up, the builder will suffer loss but yet will be saved—even though only as one escaping through the flames. Don't you know that you yourselves are God's temple and that God's Spirit dwells in your midst? If anyone destroys God's temple, God will destroy that person; for God's temple is sacred, and you together are that temple.

Do not deceive yourselves. If any of you think you are wise by the standards of this age, you should become "fools" so that you may become wise. For the wisdom of this world is foolishness in God's sight. As it is written: "He catches the wise in their craftiness"; and again, "The Lord knows that the thoughts of the wise are futile." So then, no more boasting about human leaders! All things are yours, whether Paul or Apollos or Cephas or the world or life or death or the present or the future—all are yours, and you are of Christ, and Christ is of God.

This, then, is how you ought to regard us: as servants of Christ and as those entrusted with the mysteries God has revealed. Now it is required that those who have been given a trust must prove faithful. I care very little if I am judged by you or by any human court; indeed, I do not even judge myself. My conscience is clear, but that does not make me innocent. It is the Lord who judges me. Therefore judge nothing before the appointed time; wait until the Lord comes. He will bring to light what is hidden in darkness and will expose the motives of the heart. At that time each will receive their praise from God. Now, brothers and sisters, I have applied these things to myself and Apollos for your benefit, so that you may learn from us the meaning of the saying, "Do not go beyond what is written." Then you will not be puffed up in being a follower of one of us over against the other. For who makes you different from anyone else? What do you have that you did not receive? And if you did receive it, why do you boast as though you did not?

Already you have all you want! Already you have become rich! You have begun to reign—and that without us! How I wish that you really had begun to reign so that we also might reign with you! For it seems to me that God has put us apostles on display at the end of the procession, like those condemned to die in the arena. We have been made a spectacle to the whole universe, to angels as well as to human beings. We are fools for Christ, but you are so wise in Christ! We are weak, but you are strong! You are honored, we are dishonored! To this very hour we go hungry and thirsty, we are in rags, we are brutally treated, we are homeless. We work hard with our own hands. When we are cursed, we bless; when we are persecuted, we endure it; when we are slandered, we answer kindly. We have become the scum of the earth, the garbage of the world—right up to this moment. I am writing this not to shame you but to warn you as my dear children. Even if you had ten thousand guardians in Christ, you do not have many fathers, for in Christ Jesus I became your father through the gospel. Therefore I urge you to imitate me. For this reason I have sent to you Timothy, my son whom I love, who is faithful in the Lord. He will remind you of my way of life in Christ Jesus, which agrees with what I teach everywhere in every church. Some of you have become arrogant, as if I were not coming to you. But I will come to you very soon, if the Lord is willing, and then I will find out not only how these arrogant people are talking, but what power they have. For the kingdom of God is not a matter of talk but of power. What do you prefer? Shall I come to you with a rod of discipline, or shall I come in love and with a gentle spirit?

It is actually reported that there is sexual immorality among you, and of a kind that even pagans do not tolerate: A man is sleeping with his father's wife. And you are proud! Shouldn't you rather have gone into mourning and have put out of your fellowship the man who has been doing this? For my part, even though I am not physically present, I am with you in spirit. As one who is present with you in this way, I have already passed judgment in the name of our Lord Jesus on the one who has been doing this. So when you are assembled and I am with you in spirit, and the power of our Lord Jesus is present, hand this man over to Satan for the destruction of the flesh, so that his spirit may be saved on the day of the Lord. Your boasting is not good. Don't you know that a little yeast leavens the whole batch of dough? Get rid of the old yeast, so that you may be a new unleavened batch—as you really are. For Christ, our Passover lamb, has been sacrificed. Therefore let us keep the Festival, not with the old bread leavened with malice and wickedness, but with the unleavened bread of sincerity and truth. I wrote to you in my letter not to associate with sexually immoral people— not at all meaning the people of this world who are immoral, or the greedy and swindlers, or idolaters. In that case you would have to leave this world. But now I am writing to you that you must not associate with anyone who claims to be a brother or sister but is sexually immoral or greedy, an idolater or slanderer, a drunkard or swindler. Do not even eat with such people. What business is it of mine to judge those outside the church? Are you not to judge those inside? God will judge those outside. "Expel the wicked person from among you."

If any of you has a dispute with another, do you dare to take it before the ungodly for judgment instead of before the Lord's people? Or do you not know that the Lord's people will judge the world? And if you are to judge the world, are you not competent to judge trivial cases? Do you not know that we will judge angels? How much more the things of this life! Therefore, if you have disputes about such matters, do you ask for a ruling from those whose way of life is scorned in the church? I say this to shame you. Is it possible that there is nobody among you wise enough to judge a dispute between believers? But instead, one brother takes another to court—and this in front of unbelievers! The very fact that you have lawsuits among you means you have been completely defeated already. Why not rather be wronged? Why not rather be cheated? Instead, you yourselves cheat and do wrong, and you do this to your brothers and sisters. Or do you not know that wrongdoers will not inherit the kingdom of God? Do not be deceived: Neither the sexually immoral nor idolaters nor adulterers nor men who have sex with men nor thieves nor the greedy nor drunkards nor slanderers nor swindlers will inherit the kingdom of God. And that is what some of you were. But you were washed, you were sanctified, you were justified in the name of the Lord Jesus Christ and by the Spirit of our God. "I have the right to do anything," you say—but not everything is beneficial. "I have the right to do anything"—but I will not be mastered by anything. You say, "Food for the stomach and the stomach for food, and God will destroy them both." The body, however, is not meant for sexual immorality but for the Lord, and the Lord for the body. By his power God raised the Lord from the dead, and he will raise us also. Do you not know that your bodies are members of Christ himself? Shall I then take the members of Christ and unite them with a prostitute? Never!

Do you not know that he who unites himself with a prostitute is one with her in body? For it is said, "The two will become one flesh." But whoever is united with the Lord is one with him in spirit. Flee from sexual immorality. All other sins a person commits are outside the body, but whoever sins sexually, sins against their own body. Do you not know that your bodies are temples of the Holy Spirit, who is in you, whom you have received from God? You are not your own; you were bought at a price. Therefore honor God with your bodies.

Now for the matters you wrote about: "It is good for a man not to have sexual relations with a woman." But since sexual immorality is occurring, each man should have sexual relations with his own wife, and each woman with her own husband. The husband should fulfill his marital duty to his wife, and likewise the wife to her husband. The wife does not have authority over her own body but yields it to her husband. In the same way, the husband does not have authority over his own body but yields it to his wife. Do not deprive each other except perhaps by mutual consent and for a time, so that you may devote yourselves to prayer. Then come together again so that Satan will not tempt you because of your lack of self-control. I say this as a concession, not as a command.

I wish that all of you were as I am. But each of you has your own gift from God; one has this gift, another has that. Now to the unmarried and the widows I say: It is good for them to stay unmarried, as I do. But if they cannot control themselves, they should marry, for it is better to marry than to burn with passion. To the married I give this command (not I, but the Lord): A wife must not separate from her husband. But if she does, she must remain unmarried or else be reconciled to her husband. And a husband must not divorce his wife. To the rest I say this (I, not the Lord): If any brother has a wife who is not a believer and she is willing to live with him, he must not divorce her. And if a woman has a husband who is not a believer and he is willing to live with her, she must not divorce him. For the unbelieving husband has been sanctified through his wife, and the unbelieving wife has been sanctified through her believing husband. Otherwise your children would be unclean, but as it is, they are holy. But if the unbeliever leaves, let it be so.

The brother or the sister is not bound in such circumstances; God has called us to live in peace. How do you know, wife, whether you will save your husband? Or, how do you know, husband, whether you will save your wife? Nevertheless, each person should live as a believer in whatever situation the Lord has assigned to them, just as God has called them. This is the rule I lay down in all the churches. Was a man already circumcised when he was called? He should not become uncircumcised. Was a man uncircumcised when he was called? He should not be circumcised. Circumcision is nothing and uncircumcision is nothing. Keeping God's commands is what counts. Each person should remain in the situation they were in when God called them. Were you a slave when you were called?

Don't let it trouble you—although if you can gain your freedom, do so. For the one who was a slave when called to faith in the Lord is the Lord's freed person; similarly, the one who was free when called is Christ's slave. You were bought at a price; do not become slaves of human beings. Brothers and sisters, each person, as responsible to God, should remain in the situation they were in when God called them. Now about virgins: I have no command from the Lord, but I give a judgment as one who by the Lord's mercy is trustworthy. Because of the present crisis, I think that it is good for a man to remain as he is. Are you pledged to a woman? Do not seek to be released. Are you free from such a commitment? Do not look for a wife. But if you do marry, you have not sinned; and if a virgin marries, she has not sinned. But those who marry will face many troubles in this life, and I want to spare you this. What I mean, brothers and sisters, is that the time is short. From now on those who have wives should live as if they do not; those who mourn, as if they did not; those who are happy, as if they were not; those who buy something, as if it were not theirs to keep; those who use the things of the world, as if not engrossed in them. For this world in its present form is passing away.

I would like you to be free from concern. An unmarried man is concerned about the Lord's affairs—how he can please the Lord. But a married man is concerned about the affairs of this world—how he can please his wife— and his interests are divided. An unmarried woman or virgin is concerned about the Lord's affairs: Her aim is to be devoted to the Lord in both body and spirit. But a married woman is concerned about the affairs of this world—how she can please her husband. I am saying this for your own good, not to restrict you, but that you may live in a right way in undivided devotion to the Lord. If anyone is worried that he might not be acting honorably toward the virgin he is engaged to, and if his passions are too strong and he feels he ought to marry, he should do as he wants. He is not sinning. They should get married. But the man who has settled the matter in his own mind, who is under no compulsion but has control over his own will, and who has made up his mind not to marry the virgin—this man also does the right thing. So then, he who marries the virgin does right, but he who does not marry her does better. A woman is bound to her husband as long as he lives. But if her husband dies, she is free to marry anyone she wishes, but he must belong to the Lord. In my judgment, she is happier if she stays as she is—and I think that I too have the Spirit of God.

Now about food sacrificed to idols: We know that "We all possess knowledge." But knowledge puffs up while love builds up. Those who think they know something do not yet know as they ought to know. But whoever loves God is known by God. So then, about eating food sacrificed to idols: We know that "An idol is nothing at all in the world" and that "There is no God but one." For even if there are so-called gods, whether in heaven or on earth (as indeed there are many "gods" and many "lords"), yet for us there is but one God, the Father, from whom all things came and for whom we live; and there is but one Lord, Jesus Christ, through whom all things came and through whom we live.

But not everyone possesses this knowledge. Some people are still so accustomed to idols that when they eat sacrificial food they think of it as having been sacrificed to a god, and since their conscience is weak, it is defiled. But food does not bring us near to God; we are no worse if we do not eat, and no better if we do.

Be careful, however, that the exercise of your rights does not become a stumbling block to the weak. For if someone with a weak conscience sees you, with all your knowledge, eating in an idol's temple, won't that person be emboldened to eat what is sacrificed to idols? So this weak brother or sister, for whom Christ died, is destroyed by your knowledge. When you sin against them in this way and wound their weak conscience, you sin against Christ. Therefore, if what I eat causes my brother or sister to fall into sin, I will never eat meat again, so that I will not cause them to fall.

Am I not free? Am I not an apostle? Have I not seen Jesus our Lord? Are you not the result of my work in the Lord? Even though I may not be an apostle to others, surely I am to you! For you are the seal of my apostleship in the Lord. This is my defense to those who sit in judgment on me. Don't we have the right to food and drink? Don't we have the right to take a believing wife along with us, as do the other apostles and the Lord's brothers and Cephas? Or is it only I and Barnabas who lack the right to not work for a living? Who serves as a soldier at his own expense? Who plants a vineyard and does not eat its grapes? Who tends a flock and does not drink the milk? Do I say this merely on human authority? Doesn't the Law say the same thing? For it is written in the Law of Moses: "Do not muzzle an ox while it is treading out the grain." Is it about oxen that God is concerned? Surely he says this for us, doesn't he? Yes, this was written for us, because whoever plows and threshes should be able to do so in the hope of sharing in the harvest. If we have sown spiritual seed among you, is it too much if we reap a material harvest from you? If others have this right of support from you, shouldn't we have it all the more?

But we did not use this right. On the contrary, we put up with anything rather than hinder the gospel of Christ. Don't you know that those who serve in the temple get their food from the temple, and that those who serve at the altar share in what is offered on the altar? In the same way, the Lord has commanded that those who preach the gospel should receive their living from the gospel. But I have not used any of these rights. And I am not writing this in the hope that you will do such things for me, for I would rather die than allow anyone to deprive me of this boast. For when I preach the gospel, I cannot boast, since I am compelled to preach. Woe to me if I do not preach the gospel! If I preach voluntarily, I have a reward; if not voluntarily, I am simply discharging the trust committed to me.

What then is my reward? Just this: that in preaching the gospel I may offer it free of charge, and so not make full use of my rights as a preacher of the gospel. Though I am free and belong to no one, I have made myself a slave to everyone, to win as many as possible. To the Jews I became like a Jew, to win the Jews. To those under the law I became like one under the law (though I myself am not under the law), so as to win those under the law. To those not having the law I became like one not having the law (though I am not free from God's law but am under Christ's law), so as to win those not having the law. To the weak I became weak, to win the weak. I have become all things to all people so that by all possible means I might save some. I do all this for the sake of the gospel, that I may share in its blessings. Do you not know that in a race all the runners run, but only one gets the prize? Run in such a way as to get the prize. Everyone who competes in the games goes into strict train-ing. They do it to get a crown that will not last, but we do it to get a crown that will last forever. Therefore I do not run like someone running aimlessly; I do not fight like a boxer beating the air. No, I strike a blow to my body and make it my slave so that after I have preached to others, I myself will not be disqualified for the prize.

For I do not want you to be ignorant of the fact, brothers and sisters, that our ancestors were all under the cloud and that they all passed through the sea. They were all baptized into Moses in the cloud and in the sea. They all ate the same spiritual food and drank the same spiritual drink; for they drank from the spiritual rock that accompanied them, and that rock was Christ. Nevertheless, God was not pleased with most of them; their bodies were scattered in the wilderness. Now these things occurred as examples to keep us from setting our hearts on evil things as they did. Do not be idolaters, as some of them were; as it is written: "The people sat down to eat and drink and got up to indulge in revelry." We should not commit sexual immorality, as some of them did—and in one day twenty-three thousand of them died. We should not test Christ, as some of them did—and were killed by snakes. And do not grumble, as some of them did—and were killed by the destroying angel. These things happened to them as examples and were written down as warnings for us, on whom the culmination of the ages has come.

So, if you think you are standing firm, be careful that you don't fall! No temptation has overtaken you except what is common to mankind. And God is faithful; he will not let you be tempted beyond what you can bear. But when you are tempted, he will also provide a way out so that you can endure it. Therefore, my dear friends, flee from idolatry. I speak to sensible people; judge for yourselves what I say. Is not the cup of thanksgiving for which we give thanks a participation in the blood of Christ? And is not the bread that we break a participation in the body of Christ? Because there is one loaf, we, who are many, are one body, for we all share the one loaf.

Consider the people of Israel: Do not those who eat the sacrifices participate in the altar? Do I mean then that food sacrificed to an idol is anything, or that an idol is anything? No, but the sacrifices of pagans are offered to demons, not to God, and I do not want you to be participants with demons.

You cannot drink the cup of the Lord and the cup of demons too; you cannot have a part in both the Lord's table and the table of demons. Are we trying to arouse the Lord's jealousy? Are we stronger than he? "I have the right to do anything," you say—but not everything is beneficial. "I have the right to do anything"—but not everything is constructive. No one should seek their own good, but the good of others. Eat anything sold in the meat market without raising questions of conscience, for, "The earth is the Lord's, and everything in it." If an unbeliever invites you to a meal and you want to go, eat whatever is put before you without raising questions of conscience. But if someone says to you, "This has been offered in sacrifice," then do not eat it, both for the sake of the one who told you and for the sake of conscience. I am referring to the other person's conscience, not yours. For why is my freedom being judged by another's conscience? If I take part in the meal with thankfulness, why am I denounced because of something I thank God for?

So whether you eat or drink or whatever you do, do it all for the glory of God. Do not cause anyone to stumble, whether

Jews, Greeks or the church of God— even as I try to please everyone in every way. For I am not seeking my own good but the good of many, so that they may be saved.

Follow my example, as I follow the example of Christ. I praise you for remembering me in everything and for holding to the traditions just as I passed them on to you. But I want you to realize that the head of every man is Christ, and the head of the woman is man, and the head of Christ is God. Every man who prays or prophesies with his head covered dishonors his head. But every woman who prays or prophesies with her head uncovered dishonors her head—it is the same as having her head shaved. For if a woman does not cover her head, she might as well have her hair cut off; but if it is a disgrace for a woman to have her hair cut off or her head shaved, then she should cover her head. A man ought not to cover his head, since he is the image and glory of God; but woman is the glory of man. For man did not come from woman, but woman from man; neither was man created for woman, but woman for man. It is for this reason that a woman ought to have authority over her own head, because of the angels.

Nevertheless, in the Lord woman is not independent of man, nor is man independent of woman. For as woman came from man, so also man is born of woman. But everything comes from God. Judge for yourselves: Is it proper for a woman to pray to God with her head uncovered? Does not the very nature of things teach you that if a man has long hair, it is a disgrace to him, but that if a woman has long hair, it is her glory? For long hair is given to her as a covering. If anyone wants to be contentious about this, we have no other practice—nor do the churches of God. In the following directives I have no praise for you, for your meetings do more harm than good.

In the first place, I hear that when you come together as a church, there are divisions among you, and to some extent I believe it. No doubt there have to be differences among you to show which of you have God's approval. So then, when you come together, it is not the Lord's Supper you eat, for when you are eating, some of you go ahead with your own private suppers. As a result, one person remains hungry and another gets drunk. Don't you have homes to eat and drink in? Or do you despise the church of God by humiliating those who have nothing?

What shall I say to you? Shall I praise you? Certainly not in this matter! For I received from the Lord what I also passed on to you: The Lord Jesus, on the night he was betrayed, took bread, and when he had given thanks, he broke it and said, "This is my body, which is for you; do this in remembrance of me." In the same way, after supper he took the cup, saying, "This cup is the new covenant in my blood; do this, whenever you drink it, in remembrance of me." For whenever you eat this bread and drink this cup, you proclaim the Lord's death until he comes. So then, whoever eats the bread or drinks the cup of the Lord in an unworthy manner will be guilty of sinning against the body and blood of the Lord. Everyone ought to examine themselves before they eat of the bread and drink from the cup. For those who eat and drink without discerning the body of Christ eat and drink judgment on themselves. That is why many among you are weak and sick, and a number of you have fallen asleep. But if we were more discerning with regard to ourselves, we would not come under such judgment. Nevertheless, when we are judged in this way by the Lord, we are being disciplined so that we will not be finally condemned with the world. So then, my brothers and sisters, when you gather to eat, you should all eat together. Anyone who is hungry should eat something at home, so that when you meet together it may not result in judgment. And when I come I will give further directions.

Now about the gifts of the Spirit, brothers and sisters, I do not want you to be uninformed. You know that when you were pagans, somehow or other you were influenced and led astray to mute idols. Therefore I want you to know that no one who is speaking by the Spirit of God says, "Jesus be cursed," and no one can say, "Jesus is Lord," except by the Holy Spirit. There are different kinds of gifts, but the same Spirit distributes them. There are different kinds of service, but the same Lord. There are different kinds of working, but in all of them and in everyone it is the same God at work. Now to each one the manifestation of the Spirit is given for the common good. To one there is given through the Spirit a message of wisdom, to another a message of knowledge by means of the same Spirit, to another faith by the same Spirit, to another gifts of healing by that one Spirit, to another miraculous powers, to another prophecy, to another distinguishing between spirits, to another speaking in different kinds of tongues, and to still another the interpretation of tongues. All these are the work of one and the same Spirit, and he distributes them to each one, just as he determines. Just as a body, though one, has many parts, but all its many parts form one body, so it is with Christ. For we were all baptized by one Spirit so as to form one body—whether Jews or Gentiles, slave or free—and we were all given the one Spirit to drink. Even so the body is not made up of one part but of many.

Now if the foot should say, "Because I am not a hand, I do not belong to the body," it would not for that reason stop being part of the body. And if the ear should say, "Because I am not an eye, I do not belong to the body," it would not for that reason stop being part of the body. If the whole body were an eye, where would the sense of hearing be? If the whole body were an ear, where would the sense of smell be? But in fact God has placed the parts in the body, every one of them, just as he wanted them to be. If they were all one part, where would the body be?

As it is, there are many parts, but one body. The eye cannot say to the hand, "I don't need you!" And the head cannot say to the feet, "I don't need you!" On the contrary, those parts of the body that seem to be weaker are indispensable, and the parts that we think are less honorable we treat with special honor. And the parts that are unpresentable are treated with special modesty, while our presentable parts need no special treatment. But God has put the body together, giving greater honor to the parts that lacked it, so that there should be no division in the body, but that its parts should have equal concern for each other. If one part suffers, every part suffers with it; if one part is honored, every part rejoices with it. Now you are the body of Christ, and each one of you is a part of it. And God has placed in the church first of all apostles, second prophets, third teachers, then miracles, then gifts of healing, of helping, of guidance, and of different kinds of tongues. Are all apostles? Are all prophets? Are all teachers? Do all work miracles? Do all have gifts of healing? Do all speak in tongues? Do all interpret? Now eagerly desire the greater gifts. And yet I will show you the most excellent way.

If I speak in the tongues of men or of angels, but do not have love, I am only a resounding gong or a clanging cymbal. If I have the gift of prophecy and can fathom all mysteries and all knowledge, and if I have a faith that can move mountains, but do not have love, I am nothing. If I give all I possess to the poor and give over my body to hardship that I may boast, but do not have love, I gain nothing.

Love is patient, love is kind. It does not envy, it does not boast, it is not proud. It does not dishonor others, it is not self-seeking, it is not easily angered, it keeps no record of wrongs. Love does not delight in evil but rejoices with the truth. It always protects, always trusts, always hopes, always perseveres. Love never fails. But where there are prophecies, they will cease; where there are tongues, they will be stilled; where there is knowledge, it will pass away. For we know in part and we prophesy in part, but when completeness comes, what is in part disappears. When I was a child, I talked like a child, I thought like a child, I reasoned like a child. When I became a man, I put the ways of childhood behind me. For now we see only a reflection as in a mirror; then we shall see face to face. Now I know in part; then I shall know fully, even as I am fully known. And now these three remain: faith, hope and love. But the greatest of these is love.

Follow the way of love and eagerly desire gifts of the Spirit, especially prophecy. For anyone who speaks in a tongue does not speak to people but to God. Indeed, no one understands them; they utter mysteries by the Spirit. But the one who prophesies speaks to people for their strengthening, encouraging and comfort. Anyone who speaks in a tongue edifies themselves, but the one who prophesies edifies the church. I would like every one of you to speak in tongues, but I would rather have you prophesy. The one who prophesies is greater than the one who speaks in tongues, unless someone interprets, so that the church may be edified. Now, brothers and sisters, if I come to you and speak in tongues, what good will I be to you, unless I bring you some revelation or knowledge or prophecy or word of instruction? Even in the case of lifeless things that make sounds, such as the pipe or harp, how will anyone know what tune is being played unless there is a distinction in the notes?

Again, if the trumpet does not sound a clear call, who will get ready for battle? So it is with you. Unless you speak intelligible words with your tongue, how will anyone know what you are saying? You will just be speaking into the air. Undoubtedly there are all sorts of languages in the world, yet none of them is without meaning. If then I do not grasp the meaning of what someone is saying, I am a foreigner to the speaker, and the speaker is a foreigner to me. So it is with you. Since you are eager for gifts of the Spirit, try to excel in those that build up the church.

For this reason the one who speaks in a tongue should pray that they may interpret what they say. For if I pray in a tongue, my spirit prays, but my mind is unfruitful. So what shall I do? I will pray with my spirit, but I will also pray with my understanding; I will sing with my spirit, but I will also sing with my understanding. Otherwise when you are praising God in the Spirit, how can someone else, who is now put in the position of an inquirer, say "Amen" to your thanksgiving, since they do not know what you are saying? You are giving thanks well enough, but no one else is edified. I thank God that I speak in tongues more than all of you. But in the church I would rather speak five intel-ligible words to instruct others than ten thousand words in a tongue. Brothers and sisters, stop thinking like children. In regard to evil be infants, but in your thinking be adults. In the Law it is written: "With other tongues and through the lips of foreigners I will speak to this people, but even then they will not listen to me, says the Lord."

Tongues, then, are a sign, not for believers but for un-believers; prophecy, however, is not for unbelievers but for believers. So if the whole church comes together and everyone speaks in tongues, and inquirers or unbelievers come in, will they not say that you are out of your mind? But if an unbeliever or an inquirer comes in while everyone is prophesying, they are convicted of sin and are brought under judgment by all, as the secrets of their hearts are laid bare. So they will fall down and worship God, exclaiming,

"God is really among you!" What then shall we say, brothers and sisters? When you come together, each of you has a hymn, or a word of instruction, a revelation, a tongue or an interpretation. Everything must be done so that the church may be built up. If anyone speaks in a tongue, two—or at the most three—should speak, one at a time, and someone must interpret. If there is no interpreter, the speaker should keep quiet in the church and speak to himself and to God. Two or three prophets should speak, and the others should weigh carefully what is said. And if a revelation comes to someone who is sitting down, the first speaker should stop.

For you can all prophesy in turn so that everyone may be instructed and encouraged. The spirits of prophets are subject to the control of prophets. For God is not a God of disorder but of peace—as in all the congregations of the Lord's people. Women should remain silent in the churches. They are not allowed to speak, but must be in submission, as the law says. If they want to inquire about something, they should ask their own husbands at home; for it is disgraceful for a woman to speak in the church. Or did the word of God originate with you? Or are you the only people it has reached? If anyone thinks they are a prophet or otherwise gifted by the Spirit, let them acknowledge that what I am writing to you is the Lord's command.

But if anyone ignores this, they will themselves be ignored. Therefore, my brothers and sisters, be eager to prophesy, and do not forbid speaking in tongues. But everything should be done in a fitting and orderly way.

Now, brothers and sisters, I want to remind you of the gospel I preached to you, which you received and on which you have taken your stand. By this gospel you are saved, if you hold firmly to the word I preached to you. Otherwise, you have believed in vain. For what I received I passed on to you as of first importance: that Christ died for our sins according to the Scriptures, that he was buried, that he was raised on the third day according to the Scriptures, and that he appeared to Cephas, and then to the Twelve. After that, he appeared to more than five hundred of the brothers and sisters at the same time, most of whom are still living, though some have fallen asleep. Then he appeared to James, then to all the apostles, and last of all he appeared to me also, as to one abnormally born.

For I am the least of the apostles and do not even deserve to be called an apostle, because I persecuted the church of God. But by the grace of God I am what I am, and his grace to me was not without effect. No, I worked harder than all of them—yet not I, but the grace of God that was with me. Whether, then, it is I or they, this is what we preach, and this is what you believed. But if it is preached that Christ has been raised from the dead, how can some of you say that there is no resurrection of the dead? If there is no resurrection of the dead, then not even Christ has been raised. And if Christ has not been raised, our preaching is useless and so is your faith. More than that, we are then found to be false witnesses about God, for we have testified about God that he raised Christ from the dead. But he did not raise him if in fact the dead are not raised. For if the dead are not raised, then Christ has not been raised either.

And if Christ has not been raised, your faith is futile; you are still in your sins. Then those also who have fallen asleep in Christ are lost. If only for this life we have hope in Christ, we are of all people most to be pitied.

But Christ has indeed been raised from the dead, the first-fruits of those who have fallen asleep. For since death came through a man, the resurrection of the dead comes also through a man. For as in Adam all die, so in Christ all will be made alive. But each in turn: Christ, the firstfruits; then, when he comes, those who belong to him. Then the end will come, when he hands over the kingdom to God the Father after he has destroyed all dominion, authority and power. For he must reign until he has put all his enemies under his feet. The last enemy to be destroyed is death. For he "has put everything under his feet."

Now when it says that "everything" has been put under him, it is clear that this does not include God himself, who put everything under Christ. When he has done this, then the Son himself will be made subject to him who put every-thing under him, so that God may be all in all. Now if there is no resurrection, what will those do who are baptized for the dead? If the dead are not raised at all, why are people baptized for them? And as for us, why do we endanger ourselves every hour? I face death every day—yes, just as surely as I boast about you in Christ Jesus our Lord. If I fought wild beasts in Ephesus with no more than human hopes, what have I gained? If the dead are not raised, "Let us eat and drink, for tomorrow we die." Do not be misled: "Bad company corrupts good character." Come back to your senses as you ought, and stop sinning; for there are some who are ignorant of God—I say this to your shame.

But someone will ask, "How are the dead raised? With what kind of body will they come?" How foolish! What you sow does not come to life unless it dies. When you sow, you do not plant the body that will be, but just a seed, perhaps of wheat or of something else. But God gives it a body as he has determined, and to each kind of seed he gives its own body. Not all flesh is the same: People have one kind of flesh, animals have another, birds another and fish another. There are also heavenly bodies and there are earthly bodies; but the splendor of the heavenly bodies is one kind, and the splendor of the earthly bodies is another. The sun has one kind of splendor, the moon another and the stars another; and star differs from star in splendor. So will it be with the resurrection of the dead. The body that is sown is perishable, it is raised imperishable; it is sown in dishonor, it is raised in glory; it is sown in weakness, it is raised in power; it is sown a natural body, it is raised a spiritual body. If there is a natural body, there is also a spiritual body.

So it is written: "The first man Adam became a living being"; the last Adam, a life-giving spirit. The spiritual did not come first, but the natural, and after that the spiritual. The first man was of the dust of the earth; the second man is of heaven. As was the earthly man, so are those who are of the earth; and as is the heavenly man, so also are those who are of heaven. And just as we have borne the image of the earthly man, so shall we bear the image of the heavenly man. I declare to you, brothers and sisters, that flesh and blood cannot inherit the kingdom of God, nor does the perishable inherit the imperishable. Listen, I tell you a mystery: We will not all sleep, but we will all be changed— in a flash, in the twinkling of an eye, at the last trumpet. For the trumpet will sound, the dead will be raised imperishable, and we will be changed. For the perishable must clothe itself with the imperishable, and the mortal with immortality. When the perishable has been clothed with the imperishable, and the mortal with immortality, then the saying that is written will come true: "Death has been swallowed up in victory." "Where, O death, is your victory? Where, O death, is your sting?" The sting of death is sin, and the power of sin is the law. But thanks be to God! He gives us the victory through our Lord Jesus Christ. Therefore, my dear brothers and sisters, stand firm. Let nothing move you. Always give yourselves fully to the work of the Lord, because you know that your labor in the Lord is not in vain.

Now about the collection for the Lord's people: Do what I told the Galatian churches to do. On the first day of every week, each one of you should set aside a sum of money in keeping with your income, saving it up, so that when I come no collections will have to be made. Then, when I arrive, I will give letters of introduction to the men you approve and send them with your gift to Jerusalem. If it seems advisable for me to go also, they will accompany me. After I go through Macedonia, I will come to you—for I will be going through Macedonia. Perhaps I will stay with you for a while, or even spend the winter, so that you can help me on my journey, wherever I go. For I do not want to see you now and make only a passing visit; I hope to spend some time with you, if the Lord permits. But I will stay on at Ephesus until Pentecost, because a great door for effective work has opened to me, and there are many who oppose me.

When Timothy comes, see to it that he has nothing to fear while he is with you, for he is carrying on the work of the Lord, just as I am. No one, then, should treat him with contempt. Send him on his way in peace so that he may return to me. I am expecting him along with the brothers. Now about our brother Apollos: I strongly urged him to go to you with the brothers. He was quite unwilling to go now, but he will go when he has the opportunity. Be on your guard; stand firm in the faith; be courageous; be strong. Do everything in love. You know that the household of Stephanas were the first converts in Achaia, and they have devoted themselves to the service of the Lord's people. I urge you, brothers and sisters, to submit to such people and to everyone who joins in the work and labors at it. I was glad when Stephanas, Fortunatus and Achaicus arrived, because they have supplied what was lacking from you. For they refreshed my spirit and yours also. Such men deserve recognition. The churches in the province of Asia send you greetings. Aquila and Priscilla greet you warmly in the Lord, and so does the church that meets at their house. All the brothers and sisters here send you greetings. Greet one another with a holy kiss. I, Paul, write this greeting in my own hand. If anyone does not love the Lord, let that person be cursed! Come, Lord! The grace of the Lord Jesus be with you. My love to all of you in Christ Jesus. Amen.

Paul, a prisoner of Christ Jesus, and Timothy our brother,
To Philemon our dear friend and fellow worker— also to
Apphia our sister and Archippus our fellow soldier—and to
the church that meets in your home: Grace and peace to you
from God our Father and the Lord Jesus Christ.

I always thank my God as I remember you in my prayers,
because I hear about your love for all his holy people and
your faith in the Lord Jesus. I pray that your partnership
with us in the faith may be effective in deepening your
understanding of every good thing we share for the sake of
Christ.

Your love has given me great joy and encouragement, because you, brother, have refreshed the hearts of the Lord's
people. Therefore, although in Christ I could be bold and
order you to do what you ought to do, yet I prefer to appeal
to you on the basis of love. It is as none other than Paul—an
old man and now also a prisoner of Christ Jesus— that I
appeal to you for my son Onesimus, who became my son
while I was in chains.

Formerly he was useless to you, but now he has become
useful both to you and to me. I am sending him—who is
my very heart—back to you. I would have liked to keep him
with me so that he could take your place in helping me
while I am in chains for the gospel. But I did not want to
do anything without your consent, so that any favor you do
would not seem forced but would be voluntary. Perhaps the

reason he was separated from you for a little while was that you might have him back forever— no longer as a slave, but better than a slave, as a dear brother. He is very dear to me but even dearer to you, both as a fellow man and as a brother in the Lord.

So if you consider me a partner, welcome him as you would welcome me. If he has done you any wrong or owes you anything, charge it to me. I, Paul, am writing this with my own hand. I will pay it back—not to mention that you owe me your very self. I do wish, brother, that I may have some benefit from you in the Lord; refresh my heart in Christ.

Confident of your obedience, I write to you, knowing that you will do even more than I ask. And one thing more: Prepare a guest room for me, because I hope to be restored to you in answer to your prayers. Epaphras, my fellow prisoner in Christ Jesus, sends you greetings. And so do Mark, Aristarchus, Demas and Luke, my fellow workers. The grace of the Lord Jesus Christ be with your spirit.

Paul, an apostle of Christ Jesus by the command of God our Savior and of Christ Jesus our hope, To Timothy my true son in the faith: Grace, mercy and peace from God the Father and Christ Jesus our Lord. As I urged you when I went into Macedonia, stay there in Ephesus so that you may command certain people not to teach false doctrines any longer or to devote themselves to myths and endless genealogies. Such things promote controversial speculations rather than advancing God's work—which is by faith.

The goal of this command is love, which comes from a pure heart and a good conscience and a sincere faith. Some have departed from these and have turned to meaningless talk. They want to be teachers of the law, but they do not know what they are talking about or what they so confidently affirm. We know that the law is good if one uses it properly. We also know that the law is made not for the righteous but for lawbreakers and rebels, the ungodly and sinful, the unholy and irreligious, for those who kill their fathers or mothers, for murderers, for the sexually immoral, for those practicing homosexuality, for slave traders and liars and perjurers—and for whatever else is contrary to the sound doctrine that conforms to the gospel concerning the glory of the blessed God, which he entrusted to me.

I thank Christ Jesus our Lord, who has given me strength, that he considered me trustworthy, appointing me to his service. Even though I was once a blasphemer and a persecutor and a violent man, I was shown mercy because

I acted in ignorance and unbelief. The grace of our Lord was poured out on me abundantly, along with the faith and love that are in Christ Jesus. Here is a trustworthy saying that deserves full acceptance: Christ Jesus came into the world to save sinners—of whom I am the worst. But for that very reason I was shown mercy so that in me, the worst of sinners, Christ Jesus might display his immense patience as an example for those who would believe in him and receive eternal life. Now to the King eternal, immortal, invisible, the only God, be honor and glory for ever and ever. Amen.

Timothy, my son, I am giving you this command in keeping with the prophecies once made about you, so that by recalling them you may fight the battle well, holding on to faith and a good conscience, which some have rejected and so have suffered shipwreck with regard to the faith. Among them are Hymenaeus and Alexander, whom I have handed over to Satan to be taught not to blaspheme.

I urge, then, first of all, that petitions, prayers, intercession and thanksgiving be made for all people— for kings and all those in authority, that we may live peaceful and quiet lives in all godliness and holiness. This is good, and pleases God our Savior, who wants all people to be saved and to come to a knowledge of the truth. For there is one God and one mediator between God and mankind, the man Christ Jesus, who gave himself as a ransom for all people. This has now been witnessed to at the proper time. And for this purpose I was appointed a herald and an apostle—I am telling the truth, I am not lying—and a true and faithful teacher of the Gentiles. Therefore I want the men everywhere to pray, lifting up holy hands without anger or disputing. I also want the women to dress modestly, with decency and propriety, adorning themselves, not with elaborate hairstyles or gold or pearls or expensive clothes, but with good deeds, appropriate for women who profess to worship God. A woman should learn in quietness and full submission. I do not permit a woman to teach or to assume authority over a man; she must be quiet. For Adam was formed first, then Eve. And Adam was not the one deceived; it was the woman who was deceived and became a sinner. But women will be saved through childbearing—if they continue in faith, love and holiness with propriety.

Here is a trustworthy saying: Whoever aspires to be an overseer desires a noble task. Now the overseer is to be above reproach, faithful to his wife, temperate, self-controlled, respectable, hospitable, able to teach, not given to drunkenness, not violent but gentle, not quarrelsome, not a lover of money. He must manage his own family well and see that his children obey him, and he must do so in a manner worthy of full respect. (If anyone does not know how to manage his own family, how can he take care of God's church?) He must not be a recent convert, or he may become conceited and fall under the same judgment as the devil. He must also have a good reputation with outsiders, so that he will not fall into disgrace and into the devil's trap. In the same way, deacons are to be worthy of respect, sincere, not indulging in much wine, and not pursuing dishonest gain. They must keep hold of the deep truths of the faith with a clear conscience. They must first be tested; and then if there is nothing against them, let them serve as deacons. In the same way, the women are to be worthy of respect, not malicious talkers but temperate and trustworthy in everything.

A deacon must be faithful to his wife and must manage his children and his household well. Those who have served well gain an excellent standing and great assurance in their faith in Christ Jesus. Although I hope to come to you soon, I am writing you these instructions so that, if I am delayed, you will know how people ought to conduct themselves in God's household, which is the church of the living God, the pillar and foundation of the truth. Beyond all question, the mystery from which true godliness springs is great: He appeared in the flesh, was vindicated by the Spirit, was seen by angels, was preached among the nations, was believed on in the world, was taken up in glory.

The Spirit clearly says that in later times some will abandon the faith and follow deceiving spirits and things taught by demons. Such teachings come through hypocritical liars, whose consciences have been seared as with a hot iron. They forbid people to marry and order them to abstain from certain foods, which God created to be received with thanksgiving by those who believe and who know the truth. For everything God created is good, and nothing is to be rejected if it is received with thanksgiving, because it is consecrated by the word of God and prayer. If you point these things out to the brothers and sisters, you will be a good minister of Christ Jesus, nourished on the truths of the faith and of the good teaching that you have followed. Have nothing to do with godless myths and old wives' tales;

rather, train yourself to be godly. For physical training is of some value, but godliness has value for all things, holding promise for both the present life and the life to come. This is a trustworthy saying that deserves full acceptance. That is why we labor and strive, because we have put our hope in the living God, who is the Savior of all people, and especially of those who believe.

Command and teach these things. Don't let anyone look down on you because you are young, but set an example for the believers in speech, in conduct, in love, in faith and in purity. Until I come, devote yourself to the public reading of Scripture, to preaching and to teaching. Do not neglect your gift, which was given you through prophecy when the body of elders laid their hands on you. Be diligent in these matters; give yourself wholly to them, so that everyone may see your progress. Watch your life and doctrine closely. Persevere in them, because if you do, you will save both yourself and your hearers.

Do not rebuke an older man harshly, but exhort him as if he were your father. Treat younger men as brothers, older women as mothers, and younger women as sisters, with absolute purity. Give proper recognition to those widows who are really in need. But if a widow has children or grandchildren, these should learn first of all to put their religion into practice by caring for their own family and so repaying their parents and grandparents, for this is pleasing to God. The widow who is really in need and left all alone puts her hope in God and continues night and day to pray and to ask God for help. But the widow who lives for pleasure is dead even while she lives. Give the people these instructions, so that no one may be open to blame. Anyone who does not provide for their relatives, and especially for their own household, has denied the faith and is worse than an unbeliever.

No widow may be put on the list of widows unless she is over sixty, has been faithful to her husband, and is well known for her good deeds, such as bringing up children, showing hospitality, washing the feet of the Lord's people, helping those in trouble and devoting herself to all kinds of good deeds. As for younger widows, do not put them on such a list. For when their sensual desires overcome their dedication to Christ, they want to marry. Thus they bring judgment on themselves, because they have broken their first pledge. Besides, they get into the habit of being idle and going about from house to house. And not only do they become idlers, but also busybodies who talk nonsense, saying things they ought not to.

So I counsel younger widows to marry, to have children, to manage their homes and to give the enemy no opportunity for slander. Some have in fact already turned away to follow Satan. If any woman who is a believer has widows in her care, she should continue to help them and not let the church be burdened with them, so that the church can help those widows who are really in need. The elders who direct the affairs of the church well are worthy of double honor, especially those whose work is preaching and teaching. For Scripture says, "Do not muzzle an ox while it is treading out the grain," and "The worker deserves his wages." Do not entertain an accusation against an elder unless it is brought by two or three witnesses. But those elders who are sinning you are to reprove before everyone, so that the others may take warning.

I charge you, in the sight of God and Christ Jesus and the elect angels, to keep these instructions without partiality, and to do nothing out of favoritism. Do not be hasty in the laying on of hands, and do not share in the sins of others. Keep yourself pure. Stop drinking only water, and use a little wine because of your stomach and your frequent illnesses. The sins of some are obvious, reaching the place of judgment ahead of them; the sins of others trail behind them. In the same way, good deeds are obvious, and even those that are not obvious cannot remain hidden forever.

All who are under the yoke of slavery should consider their masters worthy of full respect, so that God's name and our teaching may not be slandered. Those who have believing masters should not show them disrespect just because they are fellow believers. Instead, they should serve them even better because their masters are dear to them as fellow believers and are devoted to the welfare of their slaves.

These are the things you are to teach and insist on. If anyone teaches otherwise and does not agree to the sound instruction of our Lord Jesus Christ and to godly teaching, they are conceited and understand nothing. They have an unhealthy interest in controversies and quarrels about words that result in envy, strife, malicious talk, evil suspicions and constant friction between people of corrupt mind, who have been robbed of the truth and who think that godliness is a means to financial gain. But godliness with contentment is great gain. For we brought nothing into the world, and we can take nothing out of it. But if we have food and clothing, we will be content with that.

Those who want to get rich fall into temptation and a trap and into many foolish and harmful desires that plunge people into ruin and destruction. For the love of money is a root of all kinds of evil. Some people, eager for money, have wandered from the faith and pierced themselves with many griefs. But you, man of God, flee from all this, and pursue righteousness, godliness, faith, love, endurance and gentleness. Fight the good fight of the faith. Take hold of the eternal life to which you were called when you made your good confession in the presence of many witnesses.

In the sight of God, who gives life to everything, and of Christ Jesus, who while testifying before Pontius Pilate made the good confession, I charge you to keep this command without spot or blame until the appearing of our Lord Jesus Christ, which God will bring about in his own time—God, the blessed and only Ruler, the King of kings and Lord of lords, who alone is immortal and who lives in unapproachable light, whom no one has seen or can see. To him be honor and might forever. Amen.

Command those who are rich in this present world not to be arrogant nor to put their hope in wealth, which is so uncertain, but to put their hope in God, who richly provides us with everything for our enjoyment. Command them to do good, to be rich in good deeds, and to be generous and willing to share. In this way they will lay up treasure for themselves as a firm foundation for the coming age, so that they may take hold of the life that is truly life.

Timothy, guard what has been entrusted to your care. Turn away from godless chatter and the opposing ideas of what is falsely called knowledge, which some have professed and in so doing have departed from the faith.

Grace be with you all.

Paul, a servant of God and an apostle of Jesus Christ to further the faith of God's elect and their knowledge of the truth that leads to godliness— in the hope of eternal life, which God, who does not lie, promised before the beginning of time, and which now at his appointed season he has brought to light through the preaching entrusted to me by the command of God our Savior, To Titus, my true son in our common faith: Grace and peace from God the Father and Christ Jesus our Savior.

The reason I left you in Crete was that you might put in order what was left unfinished and appoint elders in every town, as I directed you. An elder must be blameless, faithful to his wife, a man whose children believe and are not open to the charge of being wild and disobedient.

Since an overseer manages God's household, he must be blameless—not overbearing, not quick-tempered, not given to drunkenness, not violent, not pursuing dishonest gain. Rather, he must be hospitable, one who loves what is good, who is self-controlled, upright, holy and disciplined. He must hold firmly to the trustworthy message as it has been taught, so that he can encourage others by sound doctrine and refute those who oppose it.

For there are many rebellious people, full of meaningless talk and deception, especially those of the circumcision group. They must be silenced, because they are disrupting whole households by teaching things they ought not to teach—and that for the sake of dishonest gain. One of Crete's own prophets has said it: "Cretans are always liars, evil brutes, lazy gluttons." This saying is true. Therefore rebuke them sharply, so that they will be sound in the faith and will pay no attention to Jewish myths or to the merely human commands of those who reject the truth. To the pure, all things are pure, but to those who are corrupted and do not believe, nothing is pure. In fact, both their minds and consciences are corrupted. They claim to know God, but by their actions they deny him. They are detestable, disobedient and unfit for doing anything good.

You, however, must teach what is appropriate to sound doctrine. Teach the older men to be temperate, worthy of respect, self-controlled, and sound in faith, in love and in endurance. Likewise, teach the older women to be reverent in the way they live, not to be slanderers or addicted to much wine, but to teach what is good. Then they can urge the younger women to love their husbands and children, to be self-controlled and pure, to be busy at home, to be kind, and to be subject to their husbands, so that no one will malign the word of God.

Similarly, encourage the young men to be self-controlled. In everything set them an example by doing what is good. In your teaching show integrity, seriousness and soundness of speech that cannot be condemned, so that those who oppose you may be ashamed because they have nothing bad to say about us. Teach slaves to be subject to their masters in everything, to try to please them, not to talk back to them, and not to steal from them, but to show that they can be fully trusted, so that in every way they will make the teaching about God our Savior attractive. For the grace of God has appeared that offers salvation to all people. It teaches us to say "No" to ungodliness and worldly passions, and to live self-controlled, upright and godly lives in this present age, while we wait for the blessed hope—the appearing of the glory of our great God and Savior, Jesus Christ, who gave himself for us to redeem us from all wickedness and to purify for himself a people that are his very own, eager to do what is good. These, then, are the things you should teach. Encourage and rebuke with all authority. Do not let anyone despise you.

Remind the people to be subject to rulers and authorities, to be obedient, to be ready to do whatever is good, to slander no one, to be peaceable and considerate, and always to be gentle toward everyone. At one time we too were foolish, disobedient, deceived and enslaved by all kinds of passions and pleasures. We lived in malice and envy, being hated and hating one another.

But when the kindness and love of God our Savior appeared, he saved us, not because of righteous things we had done, but because of his mercy. He saved us through the washing of rebirth and renewal by the Holy Spirit, whom he poured out on us generously through Jesus Christ our Savior, so that, having been justified by his grace, we might become heirs having the hope of eternal life. This is a trustworthy saying. And I want you to stress these things, so that those who have trusted in God may be careful to devote themselves to doing what is good. These things are excellent and profitable for everyone. But avoid foolish controversies and genealogies and arguments and quarrels about the law, because these are unprofitable and useless. Warn a divisive person once, and then warn them a second time. After that, have nothing to do with them. You may be sure that such people are warped and sinful; they are self-condemned.

As soon as I send Artemas or Tychicus to you, do your best to come to me at Nicopolis, because I have decided to winter there. Do everything you can to help Zenas the lawyer and Apollos on their way and see that they have everything they need.

Our people must learn to devote themselves to doing what is good, in order to provide for urgent needs and not live unproductive lives. Everyone with me sends you greetings. Greet those who love us in the faith. Grace be with you all.

Don't let anyone cut in on you
to keep you from obeying the truth.
That kind of persuasion does not
come from the one who calls you!

Made in the USA
Middletown, DE
01 September 2021

47084544R00078